KT-578-720

Baboushka

'come in, my Roy-al Mas-ters, I'm glad to have you stay. I

wel-come you and ask you a ques-tion, if I may? Why

have you come this dis-tance from where your king-doms are? Oh,

tell me, no-ble sirs, why are you jour-ney-ing so far?'

'Ba-boush-ka, oh, Ba-boush-ka, we're fol-low-ing a star.

Ba-boush-ka, oh, Ba-boush-ka, we're fol-low-ing a star

Text copyright © 1982 Arthur Scholey
This illustrated edition © 1982 Lion Publishing

Published by
Lion Publishing plc
Icknield Way, Tring, Herts, England
ISBN 0 85648 407 5 (casebound)
ISBN 0 85648 440 7 (paperback)
Albatross Books Pty Ltd
PO Box 320, Sutherland, NSW 2232, Australia
ISBN 0 86760 422 0 (casebound)
ISBN 0 86760 423 9 (paperback)

First edition 1982
Reprinted 1985, 1986, 1987

Acknowledgments
This story is adapted from a broadcast by BBC Schools Radio;
the illustrations are also used in a Longman/BBC Radiovision filmstrip
The Baboushka Carol: Words © 1977 Arthur Scholey; Music © 1977 Donald Swann
The complete arrangement of the Carol is in *Singalive!*, published by Collins, 1977

All rights reserved

Printed in Belgium

Baboushka

A TRADITIONAL
RUSSIAN FOLK TALE

Retold by Arthur Scholey

Illustrated by
Ray and Corinne Burrows

A LION BOOK
Tring • Batavia • Sydney

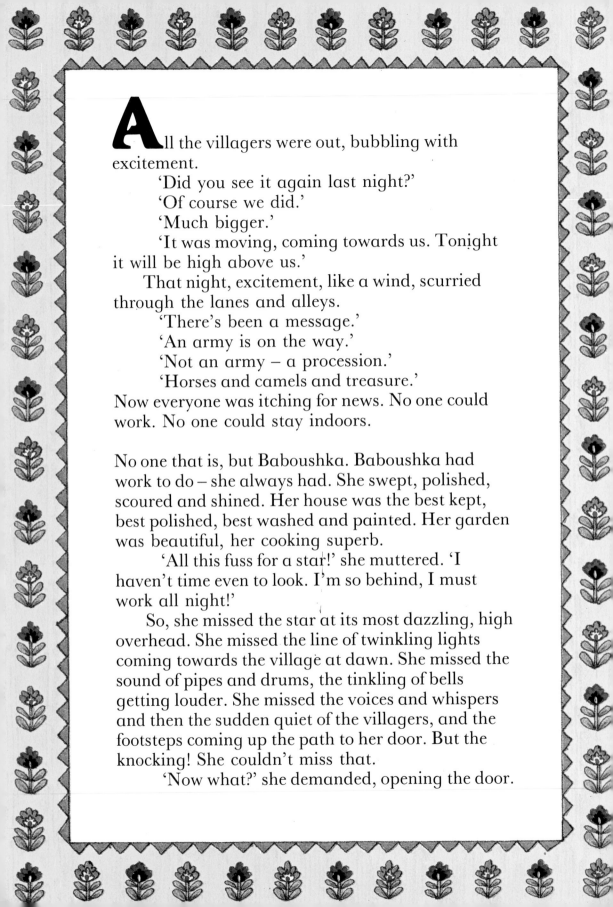

All the villagers were out, bubbling with excitement.

'Did you see it again last night?'

'Of course we did.'

'Much bigger.'

'It was moving, coming towards us. Tonight it will be high above us.'

That night, excitement, like a wind, scurried through the lanes and alleys.

'There's been a message.'

'An army is on the way.'

'Not an army – a procession.'

'Horses and camels and treasure.'

Now everyone was itching for news. No one could work. No one could stay indoors.

No one that is, but Baboushka. Baboushka had work to do – she always had. She swept, polished, scoured and shined. Her house was the best kept, best polished, best washed and painted. Her garden was beautiful, her cooking superb.

'All this fuss for a star!' she muttered. 'I haven't time even to look. I'm so behind, I must work all night!'

So, she missed the star at its most dazzling, high overhead. She missed the line of twinkling lights coming towards the village at dawn. She missed the sound of pipes and drums, the tinkling of bells getting louder. She missed the voices and whispers and then the sudden quiet of the villagers, and the footsteps coming up the path to her door. But the knocking! She couldn't miss that.

'Now what?' she demanded, opening the door.

Baboushka gaped in astonishment. There were three kings at her door! And a servant.

'My masters seek a place to rest,' he said. 'Yours is the best house in the village.'

'You . . . want to stay here?'

'It would only be till night falls and the star appears again.'

Baboushka gulped. 'Come in, then,' she said.

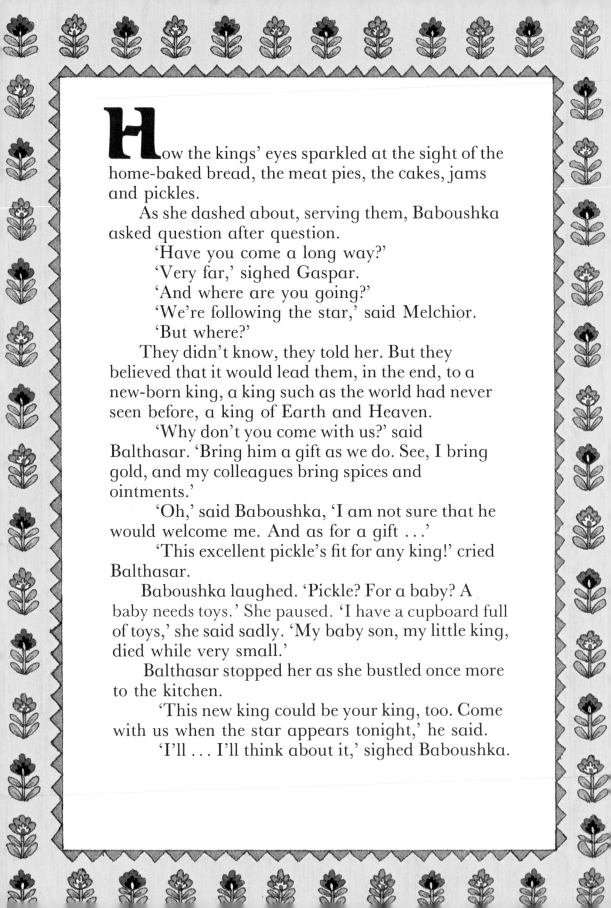

How the kings' eyes sparkled at the sight of the home-baked bread, the meat pies, the cakes, jams and pickles.

As she dashed about, serving them, Baboushka asked question after question.

'Have you come a long way?'

'Very far,' sighed Gaspar.

'And where are you going?'

'We're following the star,' said Melchior.

'But where?'

They didn't know, they told her. But they believed that it would lead them, in the end, to a new-born king, a king such as the world had never seen before, a king of Earth and Heaven.

'Why don't you come with us?' said Balthasar. 'Bring him a gift as we do. See, I bring gold, and my colleagues bring spices and ointments.'

'Oh,' said Baboushka, 'I am not sure that he would welcome me. And as for a gift …'

'This excellent pickle's fit for any king!' cried Balthasar.

Baboushka laughed. 'Pickle? For a baby? A baby needs toys.' She paused. 'I have a cupboard full of toys,' she said sadly. 'My baby son, my little king, died while very small.'

Balthasar stopped her as she bustled once more to the kitchen.

'This new king could be your king, too. Come with us when the star appears tonight,' he said.

'I'll … I'll think about it,' sighed Baboushka.

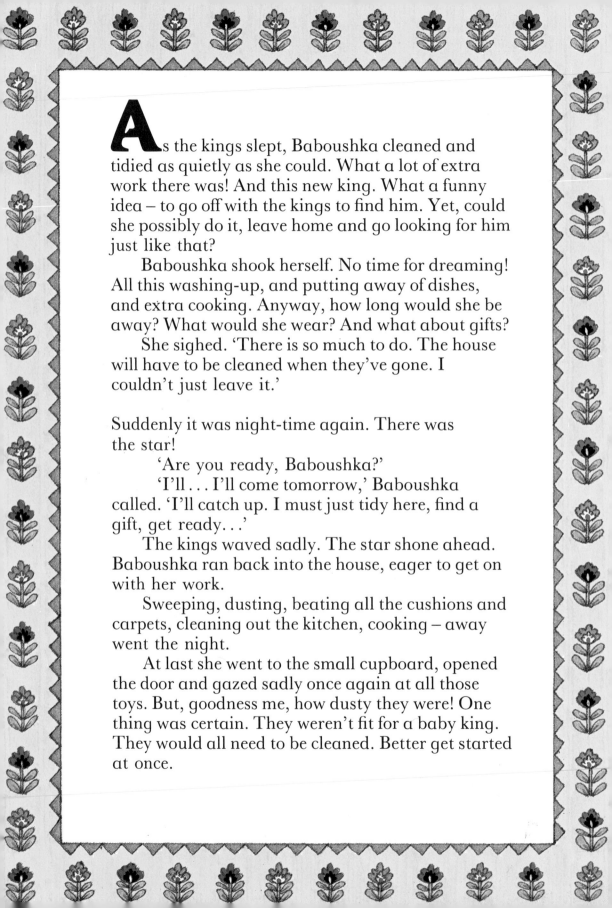

As the kings slept, Baboushka cleaned and
tidied as quietly as she could. What a lot of extra
work there was! And this new king. What a funny
idea – to go off with the kings to find him. Yet, could
she possibly do it, leave home and go looking for him
just like that?

Baboushka shook herself. No time for dreaming!
All this washing-up, and putting away of dishes,
and extra cooking. Anyway, how long would she be
away? What would she wear? And what about gifts?

She sighed. 'There is so much to do. The house
will have to be cleaned when they've gone. I
couldn't just leave it.'

Suddenly it was night-time again. There was
the star!

'Are you ready, Baboushka?'

'I'll . . . I'll come tomorrow,' Baboushka
called. 'I'll catch up. I must just tidy here, find a
gift, get ready. . .'

The kings waved sadly. The star shone ahead.
Baboushka ran back into the house, eager to get on
with her work.

Sweeping, dusting, beating all the cushions and
carpets, cleaning out the kitchen, cooking – away
went the night.

At last she went to the small cupboard, opened
the door and gazed sadly once again at all those
toys. But, goodness me, how dusty they were! One
thing was certain. They weren't fit for a baby king.
They would all need to be cleaned. Better get started
at once.

On, on, she worked. One by one the toys glowed, glistened and gleamed. There! Now they would be fit for the royal baby.

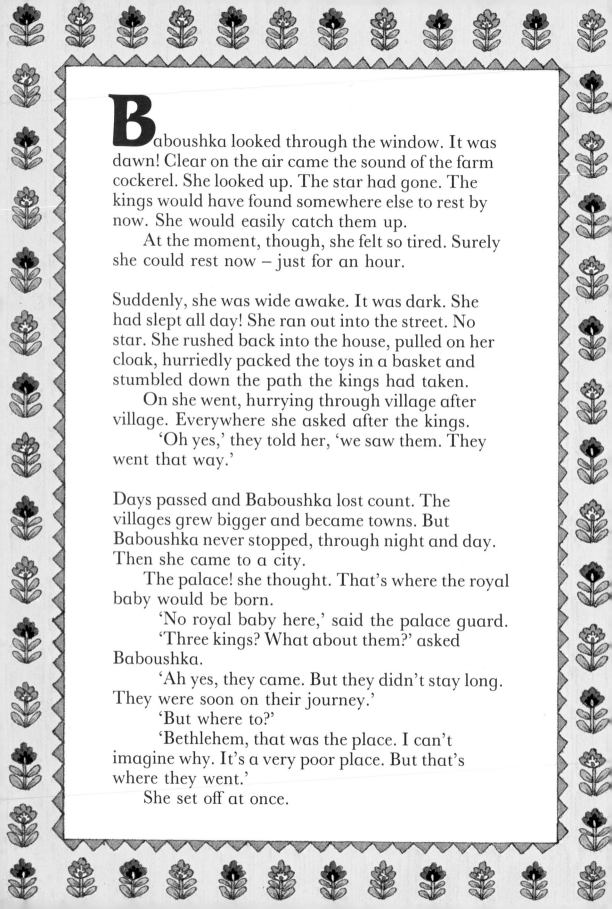

Baboushka looked through the window. It was dawn! Clear on the air came the sound of the farm cockerel. She looked up. The star had gone. The kings would have found somewhere else to rest by now. She would easily catch them up.

At the moment, though, she felt so tired. Surely she could rest now – just for an hour.

Suddenly, she was wide awake. It was dark. She had slept all day! She ran out into the street. No star. She rushed back into the house, pulled on her cloak, hurriedly packed the toys in a basket and stumbled down the path the kings had taken.

On she went, hurrying through village after village. Everywhere she asked after the kings.

'Oh yes,' they told her, 'we saw them. They went that way.'

Days passed and Baboushka lost count. The villages grew bigger and became towns. But Baboushka never stopped, through night and day. Then she came to a city.

The palace! she thought. That's where the royal baby would be born.

'No royal baby here,' said the palace guard.

'Three kings? What about them?' asked Baboushka.

'Ah yes, they came. But they didn't stay long. They were soon on their journey.'

'But where to?'

'Bethlehem, that was the place. I can't imagine why. It's a very poor place. But that's where they went.'

She set off at once.

It was evening when Baboushka wearily arrived at Bethlehem. How many days had she been on the journey? She could not remember. And could this really be the place for a royal baby? It didn't look like it. It was not much bigger than her own village. She went to the inn.

'Oh yes,' said the landlord, 'the kings were here, two days ago. There was great excitement. But they didn't even stay the night.'

'And a baby?' Baboushka cried. 'Was there a baby?'

'Yes,' said the landlord, 'there was. Those kings asked to see the baby, too.'

When he saw the disappointment in Baboushka's eyes, he stopped.

'If you'd like to see where the baby was,' he said quickly, 'it was across the yard there. I couldn't offer the poor couple anything better at the time. My inn was packed full. They had to go in the stable.'

Baboushka followed him across the yard.

'Here's the stable,' he said. Then he left her.

'**B**aboushka?'

Someone was standing in the half-light of the doorway. He looked kindly at her. Perhaps he knew where the family had gone? She knew now that the baby king was the most important thing in the world to her.

'They have gone to Egypt, and safety,' he told Baboushka. 'And the kings have returned to their kingdoms another way. But one of them told me about you. I am sorry but, as you see, you are too late. Shepherds came as soon as the angels told them. The kings came as soon as they saw the star. It was Jesus the Christ-child they found, the world's Saviour.'

It is said that Baboushka is still looking for the Christ-child, for time means nothing in the search for things that are real. Year after year she goes from house to house calling, 'Is he here? Is the Christ-child here?'

Particularly at Christmas, when she sees a sleeping child and hears of good deeds, she will lift out a toy from her basket and leave it, just in case.

Then, on she goes with her journey, still searching, still calling, 'Is he here? Is the Christ-child here?'

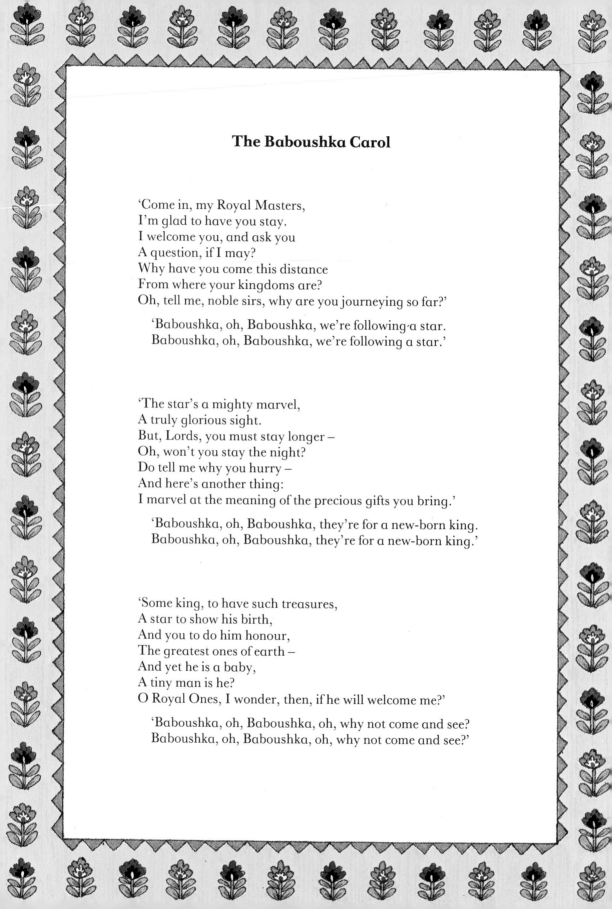

The Baboushka Carol

'Come in, my Royal Masters,
I'm glad to have you stay.
I welcome you, and ask you
A question, if I may?
Why have you come this distance
From where your kingdoms are?
Oh, tell me, noble sirs, why are you journeying so far?'

    'Baboushka, oh, Baboushka, we're following a star.
    Baboushka, oh, Baboushka, we're following a star.'

'The star's a mighty marvel,
A truly glorious sight.
But, Lords, you must stay longer –
Oh, won't you stay the night?
Do tell me why you hurry –
And here's another thing:
I marvel at the meaning of the precious gifts you bring.'

    'Baboushka, oh, Baboushka, they're for a new-born king.
    Baboushka, oh, Baboushka, they're for a new-born king.'

'Some king, to have such treasures,
A star to show his birth,
And you to do him honour,
The greatest ones of earth –
And yet he is a baby,
A tiny man is he?
O Royal Ones, I wonder, then, if he will welcome me?'

    'Baboushka, oh, Baboushka, oh, why not come and see?
    Baboushka, oh, Baboushka, oh, why not come and see?'

'I will, my Royal Masters –
But not just now, I fear.
I'll follow on tomorrow
When I have finished here.
My home I must make tidy,
And sweep and polish, too,
And then some gifts I must prepare – I have so much to do!'

   'Baboushka, oh, Baboushka, we dare not wait for you.
   Baboushka, oh, Baboushka, we dare not wait for you.'

At last I make the journey –
No star to lead me on.
'Good people, can you tell me
The way the kings have gone?'
Some shepherds tell of angels
But now there is no sound.
The stable, it is empty, and the baby Egypt-bound.

   'Baboushka, oh, Baboushka, we know where he is found.
   Baboushka, oh, Baboushka, we know where he is found.'

Through all the years I seek him
I feel him very near.
O people, do you know him?
Oh, tell me: Is he here?
In all the world I travel
But late I made my start.
Oh, tell me if you find him for I've searched in every part.

   'Baboushka, oh, Baboushka, we find him in our heart.
   Baboushka, oh, Baboushka, we find him in our heart.'